LADYBIRD BOOKS, INC.
Auburn, Maine 04210 U.S.A.
© LADYBIRD BOOKS LTD 1990
Loughborough, Leicestershire, England

Printed in England (3)

The Ghost in the Attic

By Fern Howard
Illustrated by Ann Iosa

Ladybird Books

Amy and her family were visiting Grandma and Grandpa at their house in the country.

Every year, Grandma and Grandpa threw a big costume party for all their friends. One day when Amy came in from the yard, she found her whole family trying on costumes in the living room.

Amy thought everyone looked awfully frightening. She was glad it was only make-believe.

Grandma and Grandpa kept all the costumes in the attic.

"Why don't you go and get one?" Amy's sister Emily asked.

Amy was a little afraid of the attic, but she didn't want her brothers and sister to know that.

She went to the end of the long hallway where the stairs to the attic stood. She walked up the dark, creaking staircase. Slowly she opened the heavy door.

As soon as the door was open, a fierce, cold wind swirled around Amy. A deep, booming laugh filled the air: "HA HA HA HA HAAAAA!"

Amy let the door bang shut. She flew down the stairs as fast as she could.

At the bottom of the stairs, Amy's brother Jonathan walked past her to the attic. Frightened but curious, Amy waited for him to come back.

Soon Jonathan returned, smiling. "I knew I'd find a good wizard's hat up there," he said. He patted Amy on the head. "What's the matter?" he asked. "Did you just see a ghost?"

The next day, Amy still didn't have a costume—and the party was only a day away. So, with her heart thumping, Amy once again climbed the stairs to the attic. They seemed to creak even more loudly this time.

Slowly... slowly... slowly she opened the door.

A bright flash of lightning filled the room, and a thunderous voice shouted, "GO AWAY!"

Amy went, just as fast as she could.

The next day was party day. Amy had no costume, and she was miserable. She hadn't slept all night, thinking about the ghost in the attic.

Then she saw her brother Billy coming from the attic, wearing an eye patch and carrying a pirate's dagger. "Yo-ho-ho and a bottle of rum!" he sang.

That did it! Billy hadn't seen a ghost in the attic. And Jonathan hadn't seen one, either.

"Because there *is* no ghost," Amy said out loud, trying to give herself courage. But her heart was still pounding as she walked up the stairs again.

Amy took a deep breath, squeezed her eyes shut, and pushed open the door.

This time, she heard loud, eerie music, clanking chains, and howls and whispers.

It wasn't just one ghost—it sounded like a whole family of ghosts!

Amy opened her eyes wide and tried to shout, but all that came out was a tiny squeak.

To her surprise, the ghost noises stopped instantly.

Then a door slammed shut on a little wooden cabinet in a corner of the attic. The cabinet quivered, as if something were trembling inside it.

Amy wanted to race away. It took all her courage
to climb the last few steps up into the attic.

Her legs wobbled as she walked across the room.

She shivered as she opened the cabinet door.

Out popped... a teeny-tiny ghost!

"You're so tiny!" Amy exclaimed.

"I know that!" the ghost replied testily. He was trying to kick something out of sight. It was a book called *Big Bad Tricks for Little Old Ghosts*.

"How come you didn't spook the others?" Amy asked.

"They're so big and noisy, *I* was scared of *them*," the ghost answered. "You won't tell, will you?"

"They always tease me about being the littlest and most afraid," said Amy. "It would be big news if I told them I'd met a real ghost, even a teeny-tiny one."

"Oh, please don't!" said the ghost. "What if I gave you something special, something that would *really* impress everyone?"

A little while later, the party was just beginning in the living room. Everyone was talking and laughing and having a good time. Suddenly Emily turned pale.

"Yiiiii," she screamed. "What's that coming down the stairs?"

"It's a ghost!" shouted Jonathan. "A *real* ghost!"

"Help!" yelled Billy.

Everyone stood very still, too terrified to speak.

"It's only me!" Amy exclaimed.

Everyone sighed with relief. They all agreed that Amy was the scariest, most horrible ghost they had ever seen.

"Funny," said Grandma, "I don't remember putting any costume like that in the attic."

As she spoke, the lights blinked and went out, and ghostly moans filled the room. It was a long moment before the lights came on again and the noises stopped. And Amy was the only one who was not terribly afraid.